Monika Beisner

FANTASTIC TOYS

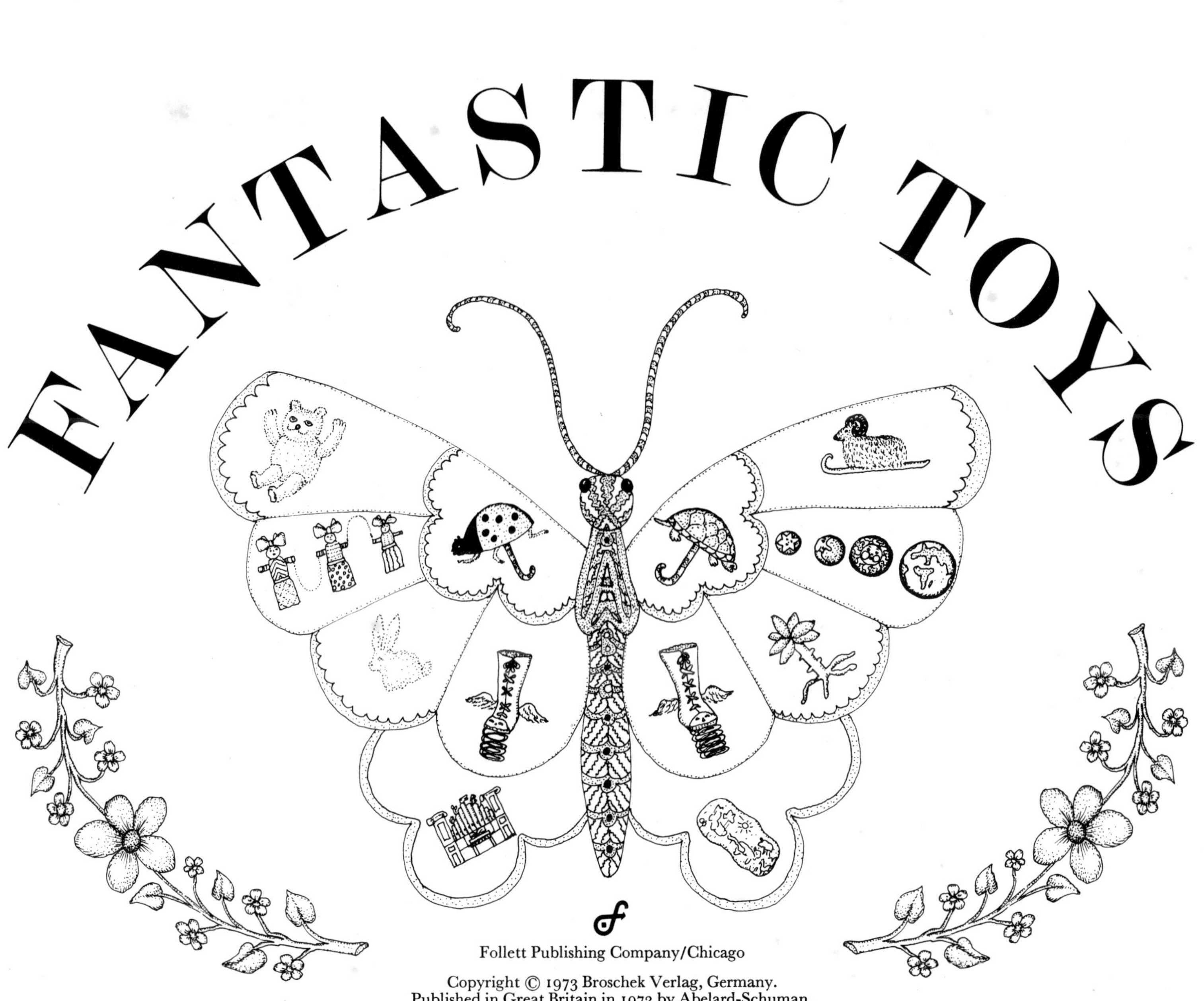

Follett Publishing Company/Chicago

Published in Great Britain in 1973 by Abelard-Schuman.
Published 1975 in the United States of America
by Follett Publishing Company, a division of Follett Corporation.

Library of Congress Catalog Card Number: 74-79249

ISBN 0-695-40504-7 Titan Binding
ISBN 0-695-80504-5 Trade Binding

First Printing

Jumping Boots

Everybody likes to jump. At last winged Jumping Boots have been invented.

The boots in the picture are green with yellow laces. Springs of precious metal are fastened to the soles, and you can bounce on them just as you can on a mattress.

Small pairs of wings which beat during the jump are fastened to the ankles. You can choose either birds' or butterfly wings.

There is a two piece Jumping Suit to match the Jumping Boots. You can also wear a cap decorated with a woolly bird to make you look more like a bird when you are jumping.

Real birds are often surprised to see creatures like this and they flutter about looking very excited.

The Letter Maze

For the Letter Maze twenty-six letters, the entire alphabet from A to Z, are scattered in a field. The letters are made of wood and each one is as tall as you are.

The game goes like this: you take a basket containing twenty-

six small letters. Then you line up with your basket and at the word "Go!" everybody runs towards the Letter Maze. There you try to match the letters from your basket with the big letters in the meadow. The first one with an empty basket shouts "Finished!".

Glowing Teddy

Anna, Bettina and Christopher are frightened of sleeping in the dark. The Glowing Teddy will be a great comfort to them.

The Glowing Teddy has fur that glows in the dark. When the light in your room is turned off at night the Glowing Teddy starts to give off a faint glow. The flowers on the wallpaper soon look like stars.

If you want your room to be dark again, you just put your Glowing Teddy under the bedspread.

The Inflatable Flower

Normal flowers grow very slowly. The Inflatable Flower on the other hand grows into a small tree in less than a minute. With it you can easily peer over the wall into the garden next door.

Inflatable tulips and daffodils are already in production and next month roses will come on the market.

They are easily inflatable thanks to the three clockwork gnomes and the clockwork frog who work the bellows.

The Sheep Toboggan

I am sure you will like our new Sheep Toboggan! You can ride over the snow on a sheep made of rubber and covered with real sheepskin. The horns are heated with a battery to keep your hands warm.

And if you press your knees against the sheep's sides the sheep will cry "Baah!" just like the horn of a car.

The Gigantic Balloon

This balloon is especially made to paint large pictures on. First you blow it up with a vacuum cleaner until it is very big. Then you can paint whatever you like on it.

You can even climb on to a chair and paint birds and flying

fish, or perhaps a jumping horse. Soon you will have a whole zoo painted.

When you have finished you can let the air out of the Gigantic Balloon and send it to an aunt who has never seen a zoo before.

Throw the Planets

Old fairy stories tell how giants used to play Throw the Planets. And now we can show you a smaller version for children.

Each child gets a ball for the earth, the sun, the moon and five stars. He has to throw the right ball through the hole in the board for each of the planets. The child who needs the least number of throws is the winner and his prize is a Glowing Teddy.

Foam Animals

To make bathtime a happier event here is some foam which you can mould into shapes. Even children who are afraid of soap in their eyes love it.

This foam, which comes in pink, blue and green, is stiffer than ordinary foam and is very suitable for modelling animals.

As soon as our special soap touches warm water mountains of foam will appear and you can start to mould animals such as foam rabbits, foam sheep or foam dogs. Our picture shows that there is even enough foam for two.